LUDLUM BESTSELLERS!
THE SCARLATTI INHERITANCE
THE OSTERMAN WEEKEND
THE CHANCELLOR MANUSCRIPT
THE HOLCROFT COVENANT
THE MATARESE CIRCLE
THE BOURNE IDENTITY
THE ROAD TO GANDOLFO
AND NOW
THE PARSIFAL MOSAIC

"LUDLUM DELIVERS CONSISTENTLY—AN IM-
PLIED PROMISE OF INTRICATE PLOTTING, AN
ABUNDANCE OF FAST AND USUALLY VIOLENT
ACTION DESCRIBED WITH GREAT IMMEDIACY,
FEVERISH LOVE PASSAGES, AND, AT THE CEN-
TER, A STRONG AND RESOURCEFUL MAN ON
THE RUN FROM SUPERIOR BUT OFTEN SHAD-
OWY FORCES WHOM HE MUST ELUDE, IDENTI-
FY, AND THEN COUNTERATTACK AND DESTROY.
... ENGROSSING."

—*The Los Angeles Times*

"THE NEW BOB LUDLUM IS OUT AND YOU'LL
WANT TO GET IT AS SOON AS YOU POSSIBLY
CAN. ... THIS GUY'S A PRO. ... YOU'RE IN FOR
A *WHALE* OF A GOOD TIME!"

—STEPHEN KING,
The Washington Post

ROBERT LUDLUM

THE PARSIFAL MOSAIC

THE PARSIFAL MOSAIC
Cover art copyright © 1982 by Max Ginsburg.
This book may not be reproduced in whole or in part, by
mimeograph or any other means, without permission.
For information address: Random House, Inc.

ISBN 0-553-23021-5

Published simultaneously in the United States and Canada

Bantam Books are published by Bantam Books, Inc. Its trademark, consisting of the words "Bantam Books" and the por-
trayal of a rooster, is Registered in U.S. Patent and Trademark
Office and in other countries. Marca Registrada. Bantam
Books, Inc., 666 Fifth Avenue, New York, New York 10103.

BANTAM BOOKS
TORONTO • NEW YORK • LONDON : SYDNEY • AUCKLAND

THE PARSIFAL MOSAIC
*A Bantam Book / published by arrangement with
the Author*

PRINTING HISTORY
*Random House edition published March 1982
A Selection of Literary Guild
Bantam Export edition / April 1982
Bantam edition / March 1983*

ISBN 0-553-23021-2

Published simultaneously in the United States and Canada

PRINTED IN THE UNITED STATES OF AMERICA

H   0 9